MERRY CHRISTMAS
FROM BETSY

OTHER YEARLING BOOKS YOU WIL ENJOY;

BETSY'S BUSY SUMMER, *Carolyn Haywood*
BETSY'S LITTLE STAR, *Carolyn Haywood*
BETSY AND THE CIRCUS, *Carolyn Haywood*
BETSY AND MR. KILPATRICK, *Carolyn Haywood*
BETSY'S PLAY SCHOOL, *Carolyn Haywood*
BETSY'S WINTERHOUSE, *Carolyn Haywood*
SNOWBOUND WITH BETSY, *Carolyn Haywood*
THE MOFFATS, *Eleanor Estes*
THE MIDDLE MOFFAT, *Eleanor Estes*

YEARLING BOOKS/YOUNG YEARLINGS/YEARLING CLASSICS are designed especially to entertain and enlighten young people. Patricia Reilly Giff, consultant to this series, received the bachelor's degree from Marymount College. She holds the master's degree in history from St. John's University, and a Professional Diploma in Reading from Hofstra University. She was a teacher and reading consultant for many years, and is the author of numerous books for young readers.

For a complete listing of all Yearling titles, write to
Dell Readers Service, P.O. Box 1045,
South Holland, IL 60473.

Merry Christmas from Betsy

written and illustrated by

CAROLYN HAYWOOD

A Yearling Book

Published by
Dell Publishing
a division of
Bantam Doubleday Dell Publishing Group, Inc.
666 Fifth Avenue
New York, New York 10103

ISBN: 0-440-40187-9

Reprinted by arrangement with William Morrow and Company, Inc.

Printed in the United States of America

November 1989

10 9 8 7 6 5 4 3 2 1

OPM

This book is dedicated
with loving appreciation to
Elisabeth Bevier Hamilton,
under whose editorship
many of these stories
were published
in the *Betsy* books.

CONTENTS

MERRY CHRISTMAS
FROM BETSY

Chapter 1

FATHER'S CHRISTMAS STORY

Thanksgiving was hardly over when Betsy and the rest of the children in the first grade began talking about Christmas. The paper turkeys and pumpkins that they had pasted on the blackboard were taken down. For a week the blackboard was bare.

Soon the children were busy drawing what they called Christmas presents. They made them on large sheets of paper with colored crayons. With scissors they cut around the edges of the presents. Miss Gray, the first-grade teacher, drew a great big fireplace on the blackboard. Then the children pasted the presents in front of the fireplace.

Way up high on the blackboard Miss Gray drew the chimney. Then she pasted Santa Claus's sleigh and reindeer up in the sky. The children thought the blackboard was very beautiful.

At home Betsy was very busy making her real Christmas presents. She made Ellen a necklace of pink beads. For Billy she made a beanbag. It was cut from red flannel so that it looked like an apple. Mother cut out a stem and leaves from a piece of green flannel. Betsy fastened them on the beanbag. She was sure that Billy would know that it was supposed to be an apple.

A week before Christmas there was a great big snowstorm. The children were delighted. They went sledding on the hill. They built forts and had snowball battles. Betsy and Billy made a snowman in Betsy's garden. They put a face on the back of the snowman's head, just like the one on the front.

When Father asked Betsy why the snowman had a face on the back of his head, Betsy said, "Because we don't think it would be polite for the snowman to turn his back on Mr. and Mrs. Jones who live next door. So now when Mr. and Mrs. Jones look out their windows, they will see the snowman's face too."

That evening, before Betsy went to bed, she sat on her father's lap beside the open fire. "Father," she said, "wouldn't you like to tell me a story?"

"Did I ever tell you the story of Little Claus?" Father asked.

"You never did," said Betsy, "because if you had I would remember. I never heard of Little Claus. So begin at the beginning, and end at the end, and don't skip."

"Very well!" said her father.

Betsy nestled down against her father's shoulder, and he began. "Once there was a little boy whose name was Claus. He lived with his godmother, the Snow Queen, in a beautiful little house trimmed with icicles. Now Claus's godmother never knew where he came from. She found him, one morning, when he was a tiny baby, lying on the hearth. He was rattling his belt of sleigh bells and kicking his little fat feet, which were covered with bright red socks."

"He must have looked cute!" said Betsy.

"Very!" Father agreed. "Now, although his godmother had no idea how he got there," he continued, "she became more and more certain as he grew older that he had been dropped down the chimney, for Claus never could remember to come into the house through the door. He even wouldn't come in through the window, but always tumbled down the chimney. When his godmother asked him why he always came in by the chimney, he said, 'Because I never need a latch-key, and it never bangs,' which of course was a very good reason."

Betsy laughed. "A very good reason, wasn't it, Daddy?"

"So by the time Claus was four years old," her father continued, "everyone in the neighborhood was quite used to having him drop down their chimney for a call. He was such a jolly little fellow that everyone loved him. He had a round merry face with cheeks like rosy apples, a perfect cherry of a nose, and bright blue eyes that seemed to dance in his head. When he laughed he bounced like a rubber ball and shouted, 'Ho! Ho! Ho!' So everyone else laughed too.

"His godmother dressed him in a bright red suit to match his red socks, and he always wore his sleigh-bell belt. As he grew bigger his belt grew longer, and each year a new bell appeared. As for his red socks, they were always just the right size for his feet and they never wore out, which was very nice for his godmother, because she never had to do any darning."

"Mother would like those socks for me," said Betsy. "Where do you suppose his godmother got them?"

Betsy's father looked at her and said, "You're not listening. Don't you remember? His godmother found him with his socks on his feet."

"Go on," said Betsy. "I remember."

Father continued. "Now Claus's godmother loved him so much she decided to give him a present every day."

"Every day!" Betsy exclaimed. "Imagine that!"

"So every night, after Claus was sound asleep,

his godmother tiptoed into his room and put a present in one of his red socks. No matter how big the present was it always fit in the sock, and no matter how tiny it was it always filled the sock."

"Oh, I know!" Betsy cried. "They were stretch socks!"

"No doubt!" said her father. "Every morning when Claus woke up, he reached for his sock and pulled out his present. Then he jumped up and down, laughed merrily, and shouted, 'Ho! Ho! Ho! What a wonderful present! It's just what I wanted.' By the time Claus was six years old, the whole house was so full of presents that his godmother had to move into the house next door."

Betsy interrupted again. "His godmother made a lot of trouble for herself, didn't she? But it must have been nice to get a present every day."

"Yes, indeed!" said her father, and he went on with the story. "Now when Claus was six years old, he started to go to school, and because he was such a happy little boy, all of the boys and girls loved him. Every morning the children marched into school and took their seats. Then there was a patter on the roof, a tinkle of bells, and down the chimney came Claus.

" 'Claus,' the teacher said, 'why don't you come in the front door with the other children?'

"Claus laughed his merry laugh and said, 'I never can remember until I'm halfway down the chimney, and then it's too late to go back.' "

"Of course!" said Betsy, laughing. "He couldn't go back if he was halfway down the chimney."

"Certainly not," her father agreed. "Well, now, one of the first things that Claus learned when he went to school was that other children did not have presents in their socks every morning, and this made him very sad.

" 'I know,' he said to himself, 'I'll give all the good children the presents that fill our house.' So he said to the boys and girls, 'Whatever you want for a present, just let me know and I'll give it to you. But only if you've been good!' "

"Oh, weren't they lucky!" said Betsy. "I hope they all were good."

"I wish you would stop interrupting," said Betsy's father.

"But I like it!" Betsy exclaimed. "I like this story!"

"Well, now," said her father, "the children were delighted, and so they began to write letters to Claus. They sounded like this:

Dear Claus,
    As you know I am a very good boy, and I should like to have a sled.
                    Yours very truly,
                        Johnny

"Claus would put the letter in his pocket, and then one night after Johnny was sound asleep, Claus would drop down the little boy's chimney and leave a sled by his bed. Soon everyone called Claus, *Good Claus*.

"One day his godmother said to him, 'Claus, what do you want to be when you grow up?'

" 'Oh,' replied Claus, 'I want to be in the present business and give presents to all the children all over the world.'

" 'But you can't run all over the world with presents!' said his godmother.

" 'I can do it once a year,' replied Claus, 'on Christmas eve.'

"And so, when little Claus grew up and had a long white beard, his godmother bought him eight reindeer and a beautiful sleigh, and every Christmas eve he piled his sleigh high with presents and dashed all over the world, dropping down chimneys and leaving toys in good little children's stockings. And because he was never cross, but always loving and kind, he lives forever and all the boys and girls love him."

Here Father looked down into Betsy's shining face, and said, "And what do the children call him?"

Betsy sat up and shouted, "Santa Claus!"

Chapter 2

THE PRESENT THAT
BETSY WANTED

O NE DAY in December Mother took Betsy
into the big city. Betsy loved to go to the
city, especially when she and Mother went on
the train.

On this particular day Betsy was delighted, because Mother was taking her to see the Christmas toys and to buy her Christmas presents. Betsy had her own money in her little pocketbook.

When they got off the train, Betsy and her mother walked along a wide street. The street was crowded with people. Betsy thought she never had seen so many people before. Everyone seemed to be in a great hurry.

When they came to the corner, Betsy saw a man dressed as Santa Claus. He was ringing a bell, and he had an iron kettle on a stand beside him. Betsy saw a little boy stop and put something in the kettle.

"Mother," said Betsy, "why is the Santa Claus man ringing a bell?"

"He is collecting money to buy Christmas dinners for all the poor children in the city," replied Mother.

"Can I put some money in the kettle?" asked Betsy.

"Yes," answered Mother, as she opened her pocketbook.

"Oh, no!" said Betsy. "I want to put my own money in."

"Very well!" replied Mother.

Betsy opened her pocketbook and took out ten cents. When she dropped the dime in the kettle, the Santa Claus man said, "Thank you, little girl, and a merry Christmas to you."

Betsy said, "Merry Christmas to you, too," and hurried along with Mother.

Soon they reached a great big department store. Inside the store there were Christmas trees everywhere. They all were hung with stars that twinkled.

Betsy and Mother walked into an elevator, and it shot right up to the top floor. When they stepped out of the elevator, Betsy saw that she was in Toy Land. She didn't know which way to look first. She could hear music, like the music of a merry-go-round.

"Oh, Mother!" cried Betsy. "There are Jack and Jill and the Three Little Pigs!" Betsy pointed to the top of one of the big posts that held up the roof of the store. Sure enough, there they were, moving slowly around the post.

"And there is Old Mother Hubbard and Tom, Tom the Piper's Son," said Betsy, pointing to another post. Betsy walked around, gazing at the posts. All of the nursery rhyme people were there, going round and round.

Betsy and Mother looked at all kinds of toys, at games and dollhouses, trains and tricycles, sleds and doll carriages. Betsy saw many toys that she told Mother she would love to have for Christmas. Each time Mother said, "Well, we'll see."

At last they came to the big glass case that was

filled with beautiful dolls. There were big dolls and little dolls, baby dolls and lady dolls. There were little boys and little girls. There were dolls with light yellow curls and dolls with soft brown hair. Betsy thought that all the dolls in the world must be there. She wandered around and around the glass case. After a while Betsy said, "Mother, I don't want a make-believe baby for Christmas. Do you know what I want, Mother?"

Mother made no reply. Betsy looked up. Mother wasn't there. Betsy looked all around her. Mother was nowhere to be seen. There were a great many people, but not one of them was Mother. Betsy stood very still. At first she felt terribly frightened. Then she remembered that Mother had told her that if she ever became separated from her, she should stand very still and wait. No matter how long the time seemed, she must not take a step, because Mother would always come back for her.

Betsy leaned her little back against the nearest post and waited. She felt surrounded by trouser legs and skirts. They were all walking this way and that way. Ladies' pocketbooks knocked against her head as they pushed past her. Men carrying packages bumped against her cap.

After a while a pair of bright red legs with high black boots came along. Betsy looked up and there, gazing down at her, was another Santa Claus. "Well, little girl," he said, "are you lost?"

"No, I'm not lost," replied Betsy, "but I'm afraid my mother is."

"Well," said Santa Claus, "suppose I lift you up, and perhaps you will see her. We can't have any lost mothers in Toy Land."

Santa Claus lifted Betsy up in his big strong arms. Now she could see over everyone's head. There was Mother coming toward her! When Mother reached her, Betsy said, "I stood still,

Mother; I stood still and I wasn't scared."
Mother patted Betsy's hand.

"And now," said Santa Claus, as he put Betsy
down, "tell me what you want for Christmas."

"Well," said Betsy, "I want something very
special."

"Very special?" said Santa Claus.

"Yes," said Betsy, "I want a baby."

"You mean a doll baby that says 'Mama' and
opens and shuts its eyes?" asked Santa Claus.

"No," said Betsy, "a real one that I can have
for a baby sister."

"Gracious me!" said Santa Claus. "That's a
rather large order, but we'll see about it."

"I would like to have a bicycle too," said
Betsy. "But if I can't have both, I want the baby
sister."

"I'll make a note of that," said Santa Claus.

Betsy took hold of Mother's hand. As they
walked toward the elevator, she said, "Do you

think I'll get a baby sister for Christmas, Mother?"

"Well, we'll see," said Mother. "Would a baby brother do just as well?"

"Not quite as well," said Betsy, "but he would be better than none."

After Betsy had bought a flashlight for Father and a hair ribbon for Ellen and some handkerchiefs for her granddaddy, Mother said, "I think you had better buy some handkerchiefs for Mrs. Beckett. She is spending Christmas with us."

Mrs. Beckett had been Betsy's nurse when she was a baby, and Betsy loved Mrs. Beckett very much indeed. Betsy picked out two pretty handkerchiefs for Mrs. Beckett. One was pink and the other was blue.

"Father is going with me to buy your present, Mother," said Betsy. "It's a secret. I'll tell you this much, though. It's something to wear on your hands."

"Oh, my!" said Mother. "Is it a ring?"

"No," replied Betsy. "It's something that covers your hands all up, but I'm not going to tell you because it's a secret."

"Something that covers my hands all up?" said Mother. "Well now, what could that be?"

"It's going to be a surprise," said Betsy, laughing.

Betsy held her presents on her lap in the train. She was very quiet. After a while she said, "Mother, why are there so many Santa Clauses?"

"Well," said Mother, "Santa Claus is the love that makes everyone want to give presents."

"I see," said Betsy. "So there are a lot of Santa Clauses, because there is a lot of love."

"Exactly," replied Mother.

A few days before Christmas Mrs. Beckett arrived. Betsy was glad to see her.

"Do you know what I want for Christmas, Mrs. Beckett?" said Betsy.

"No, I don't believe I do," said Mrs. Beckett.

"I want a baby sister," said Betsy. "Do you think I'll get a baby sister, Mrs. Beckett?"

"Well," said Mrs. Beckett, "we'll see."

"That is what Mother says," replied Betsy.

At last Christmas eve arrived. Betsy went to bed early so that Christmas morning would come sooner. Mother heard her say her prayers and tucked her into bed.

"Mother," said Betsy, as she held her very tight, "do you think I'll get a baby sister?"

"I'm not sure," said Mother, as she kissed her little girl.

Soon Betsy fell fast asleep. It seemed like no time at all when she was awake again. Betsy knew that morning had come, because she could see a little bit of light in the sky. Just then Mrs. Beckett tiptoed into the room. She was dressed in a stiff white dress, and she was wearing white shoes.

"Can I get up now?" whispered Betsy.

"Yes," said Mrs. Beckett. "Come and see the present that Mother has for you."

Betsy rubbed her eyes. She put on her woolly bathrobe and her fuzzy bedroom slippers. Father was waiting for her in the hall. "Be very quiet," said Father, as he opened the door of Mother's room. Mother was in bed. Betsy thought she was asleep.

Father led Betsy over to the corner of the room. There was the white bassinet that once had been Betsy's. Betsy's eyes were very big as she looked into the bassinet, for in it lay a tiny baby, sound asleep.

"Oh," whispered Betsy, "is it a baby sister?"

"Yes," whispered Father, "it's a baby sister!"

Betsy couldn't take her eyes away from the baby. As she stood looking at her, she heard some voices far away singing Christmas carols. They were singing a song that Betsy knew.

"Silent night, holy night,
  All is calm, all is bright
  Round yon Virgin Mother and Child.
  Holy infant so tender and mild,
  Sleep in heavenly peace.
  Sleep in heavenly peace."

Betsy tiptoed over to her mother's bed. She leaned over and Mother opened her eyes. She smiled at her little girl.

"Thank you for my present," said Betsy. "Do you hear 'Holy Night,' Mother?"

"Yes, darling," said Mother. "Holy night."

Chapter 3

CHRISTMAS STAR

Betsy had the happiest Christmas day she ever had known. After she saw her baby sister she went downstairs with Father. The house was still quite dark. When they went into the living room, Father pushed the electric-light button. Suddenly the room seemed full of twinkling stars. There stood the Christmas tree covered with colored lights and shining balls. Tinsel dripped from the branches like icicles. On the very tip-top there was a shining silver star.

Betsy stood in the doorway and looked at the Christmas tree. "Oh!" she sighed. "It's beautiful."

Then she walked over to look at the things that were under the tree. She didn't know where to start first. Everything seemed to dance before her eyes. She looked around the room for a bicycle, but she didn't see any. There were roller skates from Aunt Jane, a camera from granddaddy, a game from Uncle Jim, and a red sweater from Mother, but there wasn't any bicycle. There was a book from Mrs. Beckett.

"Well," said Father. "Aren't you going to see what is in your stocking?"

"Oh, I almost forgot about my stocking," said Betsy.

Betsy went over to the fireplace, and Father took down her stocking. It was bulging, and sticking out of the top was a gingerbread boy. Betsy found a lot more presents in her stocking. There were a string of pink beads, a little red pocketbook, a new pencil box, six pencils with her name stamped in gold letters, and a box of crayons. There were also candies and nuts and a big orange down near the foot. In the very toe of her stocking Betsy found a little silver thimble. She was delighted with it, for Mother was teaching her to sew.

Betsy didn't mind a bit about the bicycle. She guessed that a bicycle and a baby sister would have been too much anyway.

After breakfast Mrs. Beckett let Betsy watch her while she washed and dressed the baby. Betsy wished that she were big enough to wash and dress her. She hardly could keep her hands off her. She loved to touch the baby's cheek; it was very soft.

When she had finished, Mrs. Beckett carried the baby to her bassinet. "Oh, Mrs. Beckett!" said Betsy. "Couldn't I hold her just once?"

"Well, very carefully," said Mrs. Beckett.

Betsy held out her arms, and Mrs. Beckett put the tiny baby in them. "Oh," said Betsy, "she's the nicest present that ever was. Much nicer than a bicycle."

"Now hand her over," said Mrs. Beckett, as she took the baby again.

When Mrs. Beckett had laid her in the bassinet, she said, "What are you going to name this baby of yours, Betsy?"

"I don't know," said Betsy, walking over to Mother's bed. "It ought to be a Christmasy name, don't you think so, Mother?"

"Oh, yes," said Mother, "a nice Christmasy name."

At dinner Betsy said, "Father, what do you think would be a nice Christmasy name for the baby?"

"Well," said Father, "you might name her Pudding. She certainly looks like one."

"Oh, Father!" cried Betsy. "Pudding would be a terrible name for a little girl."

"Well, you can't call her Turkey, because that is the name of a country."

"I wouldn't want to call her Turkey anyway," said Betsy, laughing. "Of course, we could call her Carol after Christmas carol, but I know a lot of Carols. I want her to have a different name."

"How about naming her after one of Santa Claus's reindeer?" asked Father. "Let's see. There were Dasher and Dancer, I remember, and Donder and Blitzen. Any one of those would be different."

Betsy laughed so hard she choked on her plum

pudding. "Oh, Father, they are awful names for a baby."

"Well," said Father with a grin, "you will have to think of a name yourself."

In the afternoon Billy came to see Betsy's Christmas tree.

"I have a baby sister," said Betsy the moment she saw Billy.

"That's nothing," said Billy. "I got a two-wheel bike. It has red wheels."

"My baby sister has a lot of brown curly hair," said Betsy.

"Oh, boy! You ought to see the bell on my bike," said Billy.

"I don't know what to name her," said Betsy.

"My bike is named the Flying Arrow," said Billy.

"I could have had a bicycle," said Betsy, "only I wanted a baby sister."

"You did?" said Billy. "You must be crazy."

Betsy showed Billy all her presents. They went

outdoors where Betsy took some pictures of Billy and Billy took some of Betsy.

"Say, Betsy," said Billy, "will you take a picture of me on my bike?"

"Maybe," said Betsy.

"I'll let you ride it, if you'll take my picture," said Billy.

The children spent the rest of the afternoon playing a game.

Father kept going to the front door every once in a while. Finally Betsy said, "What are you looking for, Father?"

"Just looking to see if Santa Claus dropped anything outside," said Father.

"Did he?" Betsy asked.

"I haven't found anything," said Father, "but you never can tell. Sometimes things roll off the roof."

"Oh, Father!" said Betsy. "You're just teasing."

Late in the afternoon there was a loud ring at

the front door. Betsy and Billy rushed to open it. When Betsy did, there stood a delivery man with a shiny two-wheel bicycle.

Betsy's eyes looked as though they were going to pop right out of her head.

"Oh, boy!" shouted Billy. "A two-wheeler, just like mine!"

"Merry Christmas," said the delivery man. "Sorry to be so late."

"Merry Christmas," said Father, who had come to the door. "I've been looking for you all day. You should get a sleigh and some reindeer. You would get around faster."

"Is it for me, Father?" asked Betsy, putting her hand on one of the beautiful red wheels.

"Yes, Betsy, it's for you," said Father.

"Oh, Father," said Betsy, "a baby sister and a bike too! It's wonderful!"

That evening Betsy was sitting on Father's lap. He was reading her Christmas book out

loud. Betsy listened to every word. After a while she looked up at the Christmas tree. She began at the bottom and gazed at each branch. At last her eyes rested on the beautiful star on the very top. It seemed to twinkle at her.

"Father," cried Betsy, "I know what I'm going to name the baby."

"What?" said Father.

"I'm going to name her Star," said Betsy.

"Yes, Star!" said Father. "Let's go tell Mother."

Chapter 4

CHRISTMAS SLEIGH RIDE

THE YEAR after Star was born was a happy year for Betsy. She loved to play with her baby sister and to ride her two-wheeler with her friend, Billy.

As soon as Thanksgiving was over, they began to talk about Christmas. When a snowfall came in the middle of December, the children were delighted.

"We're going to have a white Christmas, I'll bet!" said Betsy one day, when she was walking home from school with Billy.

"I hope I get a new sled for Christmas," said Billy. "Sledding's great!"

"Daddy promised to take me for a sleigh ride," said Betsy.

"You mean with horses?" Billy asked.

"Of course, with horses!" Betsy replied.

Billy whistled. "That would be the greatest!" he said. "Better than sledding, I'll betcher!"

A few days before Christmas Father said that he had a surprise for Betsy.

Betsy shouted, "I bet I know! It's the sleigh ride you promised!"

"Yes," said Father. "If the snow lasts, I've

arranged for a sleighing party. It will be on Christmas eve. You can invite five of the children from school."

"Oh, Father!" cried Betsy. "That's wonderful! Will we go sleighing in the park?"

"Yes," said Father, "in the park."

Betsy invited Billy and Ellen and Christopher, Mary Lou and Peter. They were just as excited as Betsy was.

"Oh, boy!" said Billy. "I've never been for a sleigh ride, but every Christmas I wish I could go sleigh riding with Santa Claus."

"Oh, Billy!" said Ellen. "Nobody could ever go sleigh riding with Santa Claus."

When Christmas eve arrived, the snow was still on the roads. It was frozen and so hard that it was shiny and made a squeaky noise. The night was clear, and the stars seemed brighter than ever to Betsy.

By seven o'clock the children were all at

Betsy's house. Father put them into the car and drove them to a livery stable near the park. In front of the stable there was a big sleigh with two horses. The sleigh had a high seat for the driver and two wide seats behind that faced each other.

"Now, Billy and Ellen can ride with the driver first," said Father. "Then Christopher and Mary Lou can have a turn, and on the way back Peter and Betsy can ride up front."

This arrangement satisfied the children, and they scrambled into the sleigh. Father tucked the rugs around them. The horses stamped their feet and shook their heads. The sleigh bells jingled.

"Are you going to drive the sleigh, Father?" asked Betsy.

"Oh, my, no!" said Father, as he climbed into the back seat beside Betsy. "The driver will be here in a moment."

"I wish we were going for a sleigh ride with Santa Claus," said Billy.

"Don't be silly!" said Ellen.

No sooner had Billy spoken than the door of the stable opened. Who should walk out but Santa Claus! He was wearing a bright red suit and cap trimmed with fur, and he had on high black boots. The sleigh bells around his waist jingled as he walked.

"Hello, boys and girls!" he shouted. "So you're going for a ride with me tonight!"

The children hardly could believe their eyes. They were speechless as Santa Claus climbed up into the driver's seat and took the reins in his hand.

"Gee up!" said Santa Claus to the horses. The sleigh started with a lurch. They were off!

Billy was the first to find his tongue. He said, "Are you really Santa Claus?"

"Sure, me boy, I'm his twin brother," replied

Santa Claus, "and just as good. He'd 'a' come himself, but he's having a big night tonight getting up and down chimneys."

"Do you live at the North Pole?" asked Mary Lou.

"Not me!" said Santa Claus. "It's too cold. My whiskers freeze."

"Don't you have to help your brother on Christmas eve?" asked Christopher.

"No," replied Santa Claus, "I never was any good getting up and down chimneys. Always seemed sort of roundabout to me, but me brother's all for it. Did it even as a little fellow. Never would come in through the door like other folks. It was the chimney for him from the first."

Betsy laughed and squeezed her father's hand.

The children laughed very hard and asked a great many questions. They were driving through the park now. The night was very quiet. There was no sound except for the sleigh bells. Betsy looked up at the tall trees. The stars peeped between the branches and winked at her. In the distance she could hear other sleigh bells. She burrowed down into the warm rugs and held Father's hand. She felt all happy inside. Betsy hadn't known that a sleigh ride could be so wonderful.

"Let's sing 'Jingle Bells,' " shouted Billy.

They all sang:

> "Jingle bells, jingle bells,
> Jingle all the way,
> Oh, what fun it is to ride
> In a one-horse open sleigh."

"Let's sing, 'Two-horse open sleigh,' " said Christopher. " 'Cause that's what this sleigh is."

So then they all sang, "Oh, what fun it is to ride in a two-horse open sleigh."

All of a sudden the horses changed their gait.

The sleigh jolted, and Billy toppled right off the front seat. He went head first into a big snow-drift.

"Whoa!" cried Santa Claus, as he pulled up the horses.

The sleigh stopped, and Betsy's father jumped down. He ran back to Billy. The children turned around to look for Billy. All that they could see were two legs covered with dark green snow-pants sticking out of the snowdrift. The legs were kicking furiously.

In a moment Father had pulled Billy out. He looked very much like the snowman in Betsy's garden. Father brushed him off, and they ran back to the sleigh.

"I fell out," said Billy, when he reached the sleigh.

"You don't mean to tell me!" said Santa Claus. "Sure, and I thought you were practicing div-ing."

The children changed places in the sleigh. Christopher and Mary Lou sat up with Santa Claus while Billy and Ellen took their seats in the back of the sleigh.

"It's funny," said Christopher to Santa Claus, "but you talk just like Mr. Kilpatrick."

"Yes, you do," cried the rest of the children, "just exactly like Mr. Kilpatrick."

"And who may Mr. Kilpatrick be?" asked Santa Claus.

"Mr. Kilpatrick is the policeman who takes us across the street near our school," said Betsy.

"Oh, that fellow!" shouted Santa Claus. "Sure, I've seen him often. He's got a face like a dish of turnips and hair the color of carrots."

The children laughed. "I don't think it's nice of you to talk about Mr. Kilpatrick that way," said Ellen.

"Sure, there's nobody with a better right," said Santa Claus.

"I think you *are* Mr. Kilpatrick," said Mary Lou.

" 'Kilpatrick,' what a name!" said Santa Claus. "Upon my word, I've killed flies and I've killed mosquitoes and one or two centipedes, but never have I killed any Patrick."

The children shouted with laughter.

By this time the sleigh had reached a house. It stood by the road under tall trees. Lights shone from the windows. It was an old inn.

Santa Claus stopped the sleigh, and everyone climbed down. A boy in the yard led the horses to a shed nearby. He put blankets over them.

Santa Claus led the way into the inn. There was a fire roaring in the fireplace. In front of the fireplace there was a table. They all sat down at the table. Santa Claus sat at the head of the table.

"Are we going to have something to eat?" asked Billy.

"We certainly are," said Santa Claus. "What do you want to eat, Billy?"

"Hot dogs," shouted Billy at the top of his voice.

"Yes, hot dogs!" shouted the children.

After the children ate their hot dogs and drank big cups of cocoa, they went out to the sleigh. They felt all warmed up.

When they were settled, with Betsy and Peter on the front seat with Santa Claus, they started for home.

"Jingle, jingle, jingle," went the sleigh bells. "Trot, trot, trot," went the horses' feet.

Santa Claus joked with the children again on the way back to the stable. There the children climbed out. They shook hands with Santa Claus and thanked him for the lovely sleigh ride.

Before they got into Father's car, they cried, "Good night, Santa Claus! Good night and merry Christmas!"

"Merry Christmas!" shouted Santa Claus. "Remember me to Mr. Kilpatrick!"

"Sure!" shouted Billy. "Remember me to your twin brother."

Father dropped the children off, one by one, at their homes.

"Good night!" they each called. "Thank you and a merry Christmas!"

When Betsy kissed Father good night, she said, "Father, was Santa Claus Mr. Kilpatrick?"

Father laughed. "Well, what do you think?" he said.

Chapter 5

THE SANTA CLAUS PARADE

WHEN STAR was four years old, her friends, Lillybell and Rickie, went off to kindergarten in September. Every morning Star watched them go by the house. She played by herself until they came home and told her what they had done during the day. Star knew kindergarten would be fun, but because her birthday came at the end of the year, she had to wait until the next term before she could go, and she found waiting very hard.

By the middle of November, the days were still sunshiny and the sun was still warm. It was hard to believe that Thanksgiving would soon be there. Star's little friends were looking forward to Thanksgiving Day, not just because there would be turkey, but because there would be a parade—the Santa Claus parade.

Every year the big stores in the town had a parade. So on Thanksgiving morning all the children stood on the sidewalk and watched for Santa Claus to pass by. But this year many of the children would be in the parade.

One day Rickie and Lillybell came to play with Star after school. "The kindergarten is going to be in the Santa Claus parade on Thanksgiving Day," said Rickie.

"You mean you're going to walk in the street?" asked Star.

"Oh, no!" said Rickie. "We're going to be on a float."

"How can you float in a parade?" said Star. "You have to have water to float."

"This is going to be the Old Woman Who Lived in a Shoe float," said Lillybell.

"But where is the shoe going to float?" said Star.

"It isn't going to float," said Rickie. "It's a float."

"But where is the water?" asked Star.

"There isn't any water," shouted Rickie. "I told you, it isn't going to float."

"You said it *was* going to float," said Star.

"I did not," yelled Rickie. "I said it was going to *be* a float."

"Well, there isn't any water," said Star. "So it can't float without water."

"It's a float. It's a float," shouted Rickie.

"It is not," shouted Star. "There isn't any water."

"What are you two quarreling about?" asked Betsy, who had just come home from school.

"Rickie says he's going to be in the Santa Claus parade. He says the Old Woman Who Lived in a Shoe is going to float, and there isn't any water for her shoe to float in, is there, Betsy?"

"Oh," said Betsy, "this is a different kind of a float, Star. The float that Rickie means is a great big platform on a truck. The Old Woman Who Lived in a Shoe will ride on the platform with all her children around her on the float."

"See!" said Rickie. "Didn't I tell you?"

"I'm going to be on a float, too," said Betsy.

"What are you going to be?" Star asked.

"I'm going to be on the Mother Goose float. I'm going to be Mary, Mary, Quite Contrary. I'm going to carry a watering can. And Billy Porter is going to be Little Jack Horner."

"Who's going to be Mother Goose?" asked Star.

"Nobody," said Betsy. "Mother Goose is going to be a great, big goose made out of something. Paper, I guess, or maybe cloth."

"What's Eddie Wilson going to be?" Star asked.

"Oh, Eddie's going to be on one of the fairy-tale floats," said Betsy. "He's going to be Jack and the Beanstalk, and Ellen is going to be Goldilocks."

"What am I going to be?" Star asked.

"You can't be in the parade," said Betsy. "You're too little."

"If you were in kindergarten, you could be one of the children that lived in the shoe," said Lillybell.

Star's lower lip began to tremble. "I want to be in the parade," she said.

Just then Star's father came in. "Father!" cried Star. "I want to be in the parade. Betsy is going to be Mary, Mary, Quite Contrary, and Rickie is going to be an Old Woman in the Shoe's little boy, and they're going to float. Only not in water. I want to float, too."

"Oh, Star! You and I are going to watch the parade," said Father. "If everyone was in the parade, there wouldn't be anyone to watch it."

This explanation made Star feel a little better, but not much.

When Thanksgiving morning came, everyone woke up to find that the sun was not shining and it was a very cold day. The sky was gray and the wind was blowing.

"Betsy," said her mother, "you'll have to wear your winter coat in the parade. You'll freeze if you don't."

"Oh, Mother!" cried Betsy. "How can I wear a coat? No one can see my old-fashioned dress with the hoop skirt if I wear a coat. I can wear two sweaters under my dress. They'll keep me warm."

"But your legs will be cold," said Mother. "If you wear sweaters instead of a coat, you'll have to wear your snow pants."

"Snow pants!" cried Betsy. "My pantalets with the ruffles have to show below my dress. What will I look like with snow pants showing? Whoever heard of anyone wearing snow pants when they're carrying a watering can? I should carry a muff instead."

"Don't make such a fuss. Your ruffles will show," said Mother.

Mother took Betsy's snow pants out of the closet and went away with them. Betsy began putting on her sweaters. A short time later Mother returned with Betsy's snow pants. On each leg she had sewed three rows of white ruffles. "There are your pantalets with the ruffles," she said.

Betsy took them from Mother. She held them up, laughing. "Oh, Mother!" she cried. "You're wonderful! No one will ever know they're snow pants."

Mother took a woolen cap out of the drawer and handed it to Betsy.

"But Mother, I have to wear a sunbonnet!"

"Put the cap on first," said Mother, "and put the sunbonnet over it."

Betsy did as she was told. The sunbonnet hid the woolen cap. Betsy laughed. "Now I guess you'll want me to wear mittens."

"Of course, you must wear mittens," said Mother, pulling open another drawer.

"Mother, I can't wear mittens. Whoever heard of anyone wearing mittens when they were carrying a watering can?"

"You must wear mittens," said Mother, "or your hands will freeze."

Mother took a pair of pale pink woolen mittens from the drawer and handed them to Betsy. "No one will know you're wearing mittens," she said. "These will look like your hands."

Betsy laughed again as she pulled on the mittens. She was dressed now, and when she inspected herself in the long mirror, she looked like a very fat Mary, Mary, Quite Contrary. No one would have known that she was all bundled up in winter woolens.

"What am I going to wear?" asked Star.

"You're going to wear your new brown snowsuit," said Mother. "I'm glad I don't have to dress you up to look like a nursery rhyme or a fairy tale."

"But I would like to look like a nursery rhyme or a fairy tale," said Star. "Then I could be in the parade."

Mother helped Star into her snow pants and buttoned her little brown jacket. When Star put on her brown pointed hood, Father said, "Well, you look just like a little brownie."

"She looks like one of the Seven Dwarfs," said Betsy.

When Star heard this remark, she ran off to the playroom and came back with the gray beard that she had worn on Halloween. "I'm going to wear this and make believe I'm a dwarf," she said.

"Very well," said Father, "but come along. We have to take Betsy over to the school, where they are making up the floats."

Star and Betsy climbed into the car beside their father and off they went.

When they reached the school, there were a great many boys and girls in the school yard. A very fat Jack and the Beanstalk was chasing a roly-poly Little Boy Blue. Little Jack Horner had so many clothes on that his coat had been slit up the back and fastened to a warm jacket underneath with big safety pins. But they would not show when he sat in his corner. Little Red Ridinghood looked like a big rubber ball, and Jack and Jill were wearing so many clothes they hardly could waddle.

Lined up by the curb were ten coal trucks, each with a big platform fastened on top of it. Big letters on the sides of the trucks told what each float was. Betsy was lifted up on the one that said, *Mother Goose*.

The Seven Dwarfs, looking like fat brown chestnuts, were waiting eagerly at their float. Star and her father were standing beside the driver's seat. One by one the little dwarfs were lifted up by the driver. Up they went—one, two, three, four, five, six, seven.

After the driver had lifted the seventh little dwarf up on the float, he looked at Star. "Oh, here's another one," he said. And he picked up Star and placed her on the float with the other dwarfs.

Star's eyes were big with surprise as she looked down at Father. Father was laughing. As the float moved off, Father waved his hand and called, "Have a good time, Star. You're in the parade after all."

Star waved back and called, "I'm floating, Father. I'm floating."

And that is how it happened that there were eight little dwarfs instead of seven little dwarfs in the Santa Claus parade.

Chapter 6

A PRESENT FOR
SANTA CLAUS

THERE WERE many signs that Christmas
soon would be here. At night the main
street looked like fairyland. Tiny electric lights
were strung all over the branches of the bare

trees. The children talked of Santa Claus and when they would go to see him.

One Saturday morning when Star came into the kitchen for her breakfast, she said to her mother, "Today's the day, isn't it? I'm going to see Santa Claus!"

"That's right," her mother replied.

"When will we go?" Star asked, as she sat down to eat her bowl of oatmeal.

"We'll go as soon as I finish clearing up the kitchen," her mother replied.

"Is Betsy coming?" Star asked, stirring her cup of cocoa.

"No, Betsy is having lunch at Ellen's," her mother answered.

"Where will we have lunch?" Star asked.

"At the store," her mother replied.

"Oh, that will be fun," said Star.

As soon as Star finished her breakfast, she said, "I'll put my things on and feed the turtles."

Star had two turtles that she had named Mabel and Marble.

"Don't hurry!" her mother called, as Star ran up the stairs. "I still have a lot to do."

Star went into her room. She kept her turtles in a glass tank. There was a stone in the tank and a little water. In the winter the turtles didn't care to swim; they just liked to sit on the stone. Star looked at the turtles, and said, "It's time for your breakfast." She picked up a box of turtle food and sprinkled it around the turtles. Then she scratched their backs, and said, "Now eat your breakfast. I'm going to see Santa Claus."

When Star and her mother were ready to leave, Star was wearing her blue snow pants and her warm red jacket and cap. Just as her mother opened the door, Star cried out, "Oh, Mommy! I haven't any present for Santa Claus."

Her mother closed the door, to keep the cold air from coming in. "You don't take a present to Santa Claus, Star," she said. "Santa Claus brings presents to you."

"Oh, but I want a present for him," said Star.

"Now, Star!" said her mother. "Nobody takes presents to Santa Claus."

"But it's Christmas," said Star. "Everybody takes everybody a present."

"Everybody does not take everybody a present," said her mother. "Now, come along."

Star shook her head. "Everybody should take Santa Claus a present, because he gives presents to everybody's children. I have to take him a present. Maybe he's like me. Maybe it's his birthday."

Star's mother sat down on the chair beside the door. She held her head, and said, "Darling! It is *not* Santa Claus's birthday. You don't have a present for him, you don't need a present for him, and he doesn't want a present."

"Everybody wants presents, Mommy," said

Star, almost in tears. "I'll go find something." She darted up the stairs.

She wasn't gone long. When she came down she had a satisfied look on her face. "I'm going to give Mabel to Santa Claus," she said.

"Mabel!" her mother exclaimed. "What will Santa Claus do with Mabel?"

"He'll love Mabel," Star replied.

Star's mother shook her head. "Come along," she said, opening the door.

"Are we going on the bus?" Star asked.

"Yes," her mother replied, taking Star's hand and hurrying her to the bus stop.

When they were seated in the bus, her mother said, "Where is Mabel?"

"In my pocket," Star replied. "In the pocket of my snow pants."

"I hope Mabel's happy in your pocket," her mother said. "It doesn't seem to be the best place for a little turtle."

"She's all right," said Star. "I put my hand in and tickle her every once in a while. Mabel likes being tickled."

"You're sure you want to give her away?" her mother asked. "You've been very fond of your turtles."

"Well, I didn't have time to find anything else for a present for Santa Claus," said Star, "so I went over to Mabel and I said, 'Mabel, you're going to be a present for Santa Claus.' Then I said, 'I guess you don't know about Santa Claus, but he's not a turtle.' "

Star looked up at her mother. "I wanted Mabel to know that he isn't a turtle, so she won't be surprised when she sees him. I told her he's a sort of magic person. And you know something, Mommy?"

"What?" her mother asked.

"Well, once in a fairy story a frog got turned into a handsome prince, so maybe Santa Claus can turn Mabel into a beautiful princess." Star turned and gazed out the window. "She'd be Princess Mabel!" she said with a sigh.

Star's mother sighed, too. Then she said, "I don't believe turning turtles into princesses is exactly Santa Claus's line. He's very busy in the toy business."

Star poked her finger into her pocket and tickled Mabel. "Well, I think I'll call her Princess Mabel anyway."

When Star and her mother reached the store, they went directly to the toy department, where they found Santa Claus. Star stood holding her mother's hand and stared at Santa Claus. There he sat in a big chair on a platform. He looked magnificent in his bright red suit trimmed with white fur, his shiny black boots, and his belt of sleigh bells. Every time he moved the bells jingled. His white hair stuck out from under his red cap, and his shiny white beard fluffed out over his broad chest. He held a little boy on his knee. Star saw the boy whisper into Santa Claus's ear, and she saw Santa Claus's white teeth when he laughed and put the little boy down.

There were several children standing in a line waiting to speak to Santa Claus. Star's mother took her to the end of the line, and said, "You wait here until it's your turn to speak to Santa Claus."

"You'll wait with me, won't you, Mommy?" Star asked.

"I'll stand nearby," her mother replied.

"Where shall I put my present for Santa Claus?" Star asked. "He doesn't have any Christmas tree."

"Well, you certainly couldn't hang Mabel on a Christmas tree, even if he had one," said her mother. "You see, Star, none of these children have presents for Santa Claus."

"That's because they forgot," said Star, as she moved forward in the line.

Star watched as the children ahead of her reached Santa Claus. Some he took on his lap and some stood by his knee. When the little boy ahead of her began to talk to Santa Claus, Star put her hand into her pocket. She was surprised, for she couldn't find Mabel. She thought perhaps she had forgotten which pocket she had put her in, so she dug into her other one. Mabel was not there.

Now the little boy had gone, and Santa Claus was beckoning to Star. She still was poking around in her pocket, when she reached his knee.

"Hello!" said Santa Claus, in his big cheery voice. "What's your name?"

"I'm Star," she replied, just as her finger went through a hole in her pocket.

Santa Claus leaned over, and said, "What seems to be the matter?"

"I brought you a present," Star replied, "but I can't find it." Star dug down and made the hole in her pocket bigger.

"What is it you're trying to find?" Santa Claus asked.

"Mabel!" Star replied.

"Oh!" said Santa Claus.

"I guess she fell through the hole in my pocket," said Star, leaning over like a jackknife. Then she unzipped the bottom of the leg of her snow pants. She straightened up, and said, "I'll shake my leg, and maybe she'll fall out."

"That's the thing!" said Santa Claus. "Shake a leg!"

Star shook and then she jumped while everyone stood around and watched her. Mabel did not appear. "I'll find her," said Star. "She's hiding!"

Star sat down on the floor beside Santa Claus's big black boots. She felt inside the leg of her

pants and suddenly her face broke into a wide smile. "I found her!" she said, looking up at Santa Claus.

"Good!" said Santa Claus. "I can't wait to see Mabel."

Star leaned against Santa Claus's knee. "Hold out your hand," she said. Santa Claus held out his big hand, and Star placed the tiny turtle on her back in his palm. "I hope she's all right," said Star. "If she kicks her legs, she's alive."

Santa Claus's great big head in his red cap bent over his hand as Star leaned against him. Their heads were together as they watched to see if Mabel would kick her legs. Suddenly Star cried out, "She's alive! Mabel's alive!"

"Sure enough!" said Santa Claus. "She's alive and kicking!"

Star looked up into Santa Claus's face. "I'm sorry I couldn't wrap up your present," she said. "You don't mind if Mabel isn't wrapped up, do you?"

Santa Claus drew Star to him and gave her a great big hug. "I never had a nicer present than Mabel," he said. "Thank you and a merry Christmas to you."

As she walked away, Star turned and looked back at Santa Claus. He waved his hand. Star waved too and called back, "Mabel likes hamburger! Just a teenie weenie bit, of course."

"I'll remember," Santa Claus promised. "Hamburger for her Christmas dinner!"

On Christmas morning, when Star went to the fireplace in the living room, standing on the hearth was a beautiful doll dressed like a princess with a crown on her head. A card stood beside her. It said, "This is Princess Mabel, from Santa Claus."

Chapter 7

THE PRESENT THAT
HAD NO SHAPE

CHRISTMAS was near, and Star's fifth birthday was coming too. Star always was
mixed up about her birthday. "I was born on
Christmas eve," she would say, "so that means

my birthday is before Christmas. Just a wee, little bit." But on Christmas day she would say, "This is my birthday." The result was that Star's birthday was celebrated on two days. Because she was mixed up about the days, she was just as mixed up about her Christmas presents and her birthday presents.

One evening Star was sitting on her father's lap. A fire burned in the fireplace, and Star felt very cozy. She snuggled down in her father's arms.

"Tell me, Twinkle," said Father. "What do you want for Christmas?"

"First you have to ask me what I want for my birthday," said Star. " 'Cause my birthday comes first."

"So it does!" said Father. "We'll begin over again. What would you like to have for your birthday?"

"First you guess. See if you can guess," said

Star, resting her head against her father's shoulder.

Father began to guess. "A new painting book?" he asked.

"Yes," said Star. "A new painting book."

"I'm a good guesser," said Father.

"Guess again," said Star.

"A catalooper?" said Father.

Star sat up and looked at her father in surprise. "A what?" she asked.

"I said a catalooper," said Father.

"I never heard of a catalooper," said Star.

"I've never heard of one either," said Father, "but it sounds as though it should be something." Father and Star both laughed.

"Now, Father," said Star, "guess some more."

"Oh, my!" said Father. "This is going to be hard. You'll have to help me. What shape is it? Is it round?"

"No, it isn't round," said Star.

"Is it square?" Father asked.

"No." Star laughed. "It isn't square."

"Is it long?" said Father.

Star was laughing harder now. "No, no!" she cried. "It isn't long."

"Then it must be short," said Father.

"No, no, no!" Star shouted with laughter.

"Oh, dear!" said Father. "Help me a little bit. Just a little."

Star doubled over on her father's lap, laughing. When she managed to stop, she said, "It hasn't any shape at all!"

"What! No shape?" cried Father. "A present without a shape, Twinkle?"

Star nodded her head. "That's right."

Father wrinkled his forehead and made his face look very long. "Oh, Twinkle!" he said. "I can't think of a present without a shape. Toys have shapes. Dolls have shapes. Animals have shapes. Books have shapes. How can I wrap it up in paper and tie it with ribbon if it doesn't have any shape?"

Star buried her face in her father's neck and laughed and laughed. "Oh, Father," she cried, "you can't wrap the present that I want in paper. You can't tie it with ribbon."

"Then I give up," said Father. "You'll have to tell me what it is you want for a birthday present."

"I want to go to kindergarten," Star shouted. "That's what I want for my birthday. I told you it didn't have any shape."

"It certainly doesn't." Father laughed.

"Do you think I'll get the present?" Star asked.

"I don't know, Twinkle," said Father, "but we shall see."

"I'll be five years old," said Star. "I'll be old enough to go to kindergarten."

"I know that," said Father, "but I don't believe they'll take you in on the very day you are five. I think you'll have to wait until the new term begins."

"But they said I could come when I was five," said Star.

"Well, we shall see," said Father.

On the morning of December twenty-fourth Star woke up feeling that something exciting was going to happen. She lay very still and made believe she was not awake. She was trying to remember what day it was. Could it be Christmas? Star peeked out over the covers and looked at the footboard of her bed. No, it couldn't be Christmas, thought Star. It couldn't be Christmas, because her stocking wasn't hanging on the footboard.

Just then Betsy poked her head in the door and called out, "Happy Birthday, Twinkle!"

Betsy handed her a package tied up with red ribbon. Star sat up in bed and untied the ribbon

and unwrapped the box. She lifted the lid, and there were the red shoes she had wanted.

"Oh, thank you!" Star cried. "They're beautiful!"

Star jumped out of bed and put on the new red shoes. Then she put on her blue woolly bathrobe and went downstairs to find her mother.

"Look, Mother," she said. "I have on my new red shoes."

"Good morning, darling," said Mother. "Happy Birthday!"

Mother kissed her five times. Then she said, "Hurry up and dress. We're going over to school with Betsy for the Christmas concert."

Star went upstairs. She washed her face and cleaned her teeth. She put on her red-flower print dress. Betsy came in to braid her hair and tie her red ribbons.

"I like my red shoes," said Star, looking down at her feet.

"You must keep them to wear when you go to kindergarten," said Betsy.

"I'm five now," said Star. "Will I go to kindergarten right away?"

"I don't know," said Betsy.

At Star's place at the breakfast table there was a new painting book and a little gold bracelet. Star was delighted with her presents.

As soon as Star and Betsy had finished their breakfast, Mother hustled them into the car.

When they reached the school, Betsy went to her classroom, and Star and her mother went into the assembly room. It was a big room with rows and rows of seats. In the front of the room there was a stage with a green velvet curtain. In the back of the room there were extra chairs for the parents of the children. Billy Porter's mother and Mrs. Wilson were there. Star's mother sat down beside Mrs. Porter. Star sat on a chair beside her mother. All Star could see was the back of the chair in front of her.

"Mother," said Star, "I can't see anything."

"You can sit on my lap when the concert begins," said Mother.

Star sat still. Her legs stuck out straight in front of her. She looked at her new red shoes and thought how pretty they were. More and more mothers came to sit on the chairs in the back of the room. There were a few fathers, too.

Suddenly there was music. Someone was playing the piano. Star couldn't see anything, but she could hear the tramp, tramp of feet. The children were marching into the assembly room. Star climbed up and stood on her seat. She could see all over the room now. She saw her little kindergarten friends marching into the room. There was Rosemary at the head of the line. She could see Rickie and Lillybell and Polly. She could see all her friends.

When the children were seated, Mother took Star on her lap. Just then Miss Morse stood up in the front of the room. She looked at the back of the room, and said, "I see little Star back there. We would like her to walk up here and sit with the kindergarten."

Star got down from her mother's lap. The walk up the aisle to where the kindergarten children were sitting was a long one. Star felt much too happy to walk. She skipped all the way. She skipped all the way in her new red shoes.

When she was seated between Rickie and Lillybell, Miss Morse said that the kindergarten would sing. The kindergarten children stood up. They marched up on the stage and stood in a line. Star went with them and stood between Rickie and Lillybell. When they sang their song, Star sang too, for it was a song she knew.

When the children had taken their seats again, the green velvet curtain was lifted and the concert began.

First of all there was the song of the Christmas fairies. Twelve little girls, dressed as fairies, sang the song.

Then there was the song of Santa Claus and his helpers. Rudy Wilson was Santa Claus. He wore a red suit stuffed with pillows to make him look fat. Billy Porter, the Wilson twins, and three other boys were Santa Claus's helpers. They wore red suits too, but they were not as fat as Santa Claus and their beards were not as long as his. They all shook sleigh bells as they sang.

Star liked the song of the Christmas cookies best. Seven children dressed to look like big Christmas cookies sang:

"We are the Christmas cookies
Baked in the oven for you."

Everyone laughed when they heard the words, and they laughed at Eddie Wilson, too. Eddie was right in the middle of the seven children. He was dressed like a gingerbread boy.

When the concert was over, Miss Morse told

Star to go back to her mother. Star was sorry, because she thought she was going to stay with her little friends and go into the kindergarten room. Star didn't skip as she went back to her mother. She walked very slowly.

After all the children had returned to their classrooms and the parents had said good-by to each other, Mother and Star walked toward the big front door of the school. But instead of going out the door, Mother led Star to the door of the kindergarten. Mother opened the door and Star walked in. As she did so, the kindergarten children all began to sing:

"Happy Birthday to you,
Happy Birthday to you,
Happy Birthday, dear Twinkle,
Happy Birthday to you."

The children were standing in their places

around the big kindergarten table. Miss Morse led Star to the end of the table. There on the table was a birthday cake with five red candles.

Star's eyes were as bright as the candles. Now she knew that the kindergarten was giving her a birthday party.

Miss Morse held Star's little pigtails while she leaned over and blew out the candles. Then Miss Morse helped her to cut the cake, and Mother put a plate of ice cream in front of each child.

That evening when Star saw her father, she cried, "Father! Guess what, Father!"

"I can guess," said Father. "You went to kindergarten."

"Yes, I did!" said Star. "I was invited. And I sang. And they had a birthday party for me."

Then Star's face grew sober. She sighed a deep sigh. "Oh, Father!" she said. "Do you think they will let me go to kindergarten every day, now that I'm five years old?"

Father lifted Star up on his knee. "I'm going to tell you a story," he said.

Star snuggled into his arms.

"Once upon a time," said Father, "there was a little girl who wanted to go to kindergarten."

"It was me, wasn't it?" said Star.

Father looked at his little girl, and said, "Well, come to think of it, she resembled you."

Star settled back against her father's shoulder.

Father went on with his story. "Well, this little girl wished she could go to kindergarten. She wished and she wished. She used to swing on the garden gate and watch her friends go by on their way to kindergarten. But she couldn't go because she was only four years old. But at last the day came when she was five years old. It was the day before Christmas. Of course, she couldn't go to kindergarten on Christmas day, and she couldn't go to kindergarten during the holidays, but when school opened again, the little girl didn't have to swing on the gate and watch her friends go by. No, indeed! She went with them to kindergarten, for now she was five years old."

"Oh, Father!" said Star. "It's my present, isn't it?"

"Yes," said Father. "The present that has no shape."

Chapter 8

CHRISTMAS TREES

BETSY and Billy were walking to school one morning just before Christmas. On their way they admired the gay wreaths that hung on the front doors of many houses. They stopped before shopwindows and looked at the twinkling stars, the golden bells, and shiny balls that were used as decorations. The florist's shopwindow held a Christmas tree hung with snowflakes made of glass. The children watched as the snowflakes changed color. First they were red. Then they turned blue, green, and finally gold.

"That's a pretty Christmas tree," said Betsy. "There's a light that makes it change color."

"That's right," said Billy. "Do you have your Christmas tree yet?"

"Not yet," Betsy answered. "Do you?"

"No!" replied Billy. "But we may get one today."

Betsy and Billy watched the snowflakes change color until at last, Betsy said, "Come on, Billy! It's awful cold."

Billy lifted his face to the sky, and said, "Sure it's cold! Maybe it will snow." As Billy breathed into the cold air, he exclaimed, "Look at the smoke coming out of my mouth. Look! I'm a dragon!"

"That isn't smoke," said Betsy. "It's just your breath. And we better hurry, or we'll be late for school."

"I'm a dragon!" Billy cried, as he hurried along with Betsy. At the next corner they turned, and now they could see Mr. Kilpatrick surrounded by children. They were waiting for the policeman to stop the traffic so that they could cross the big wide street.

Betsy and Billy ran and joined the children. "Look!" Billy shouted, as he blew his breath into the cold air. "I'm a dragon!"

"We're all dragons!" cried Kenny Roberts.

"Mr. Kilpatrick is the biggest dragon!" cried Billy, pointing to the puffs of mist that were blowing out of the policeman's nose and mouth.

All the children began shouting, "Mr. Kilpatrick's a dragon!"

Mr. Kilpatrick held up his hand and blew his whistle. The cars and a big bus stopped. Then he turned his head toward the children, and with a big smile he waved to them to cross the street. "What is all this racket about?" he said, when the bunch of children reached him.

"Look, Mr. Kilpatrick!" cried Billy. "Look at our breath. We're dragons!"

"Well, get along with you," said Mr. Kilpatrick with a chuckle, "and stop draggin' your feet."

The children ran, laughing, to the other side of the street. Betsy turned to wave her hand to Mr. Kilpatrick, but he already had turned away and the traffic was whizzing by. Mr. Kilpatrick was hidden by a passing bus. "Mr. Kilpatrick is so funny!" said Betsy to Billy.

"Yes," replied Billy, laughing. "Mr. Kilpatrick said, 'Stop draggin' your feet!' "

Betsy and Billy went the rest of the short way

to school together. Billy puffed and sang, over and over, "I'm a dragon, and I'm draggin' my feet!"

When they reached the school yard, the lines of children were forming to go into the building. Miss Richards, one of the teachers, was directing them. As soon as she saw Billy, she said, "Billy Porter, lift your feet."

"I'm a dragon! Puff! I'm draggin' my feet," said Billy.

"Don't say draggin', Billy," said Miss Richards. "Say dragging."

"Dragging," said Billy.

When the children reached their classroom, Billy said to Betsy, "Miss Richards can't take a joke but Mr. Kilpatrick can."

Just before school closed, it began to snow. Billy was the first to notice it. "It's snowing!" he called out.

Every child looked out the windows. They all felt excited. In that part of the country they didn't see snow before Christmas very often. They hardly could wait for the bell that ended school to ring.

Finally the bell rang, and Betsy and Billy started off together. They lived in the same direction and often walked home with each other. "It's beginning to snow harder," said Betsy, as they stepped out the door.

"Sure is," replied Billy, "and tomorrow is Saturday! We can go sledding."

Soon Betsy and Billy reached Mr. Kilpatrick's corner. A group of children were waiting to cross the street. Mr. Kilpatrick beckoned to the children, and they hurried forward in a bunch.

When they reached the policeman, Billy called out, "It's snowing, Mr. Kilpatrick!"

"That's right!" said Mr. Kilpatrick. "My

grandmother in Ireland used to say, whenever it snowed, 'Now Old Mother Hawkins is picking her geese.'" The children laughed as Mr. Kilpatrick crossed the street with them.

When they reached the pavement, Betsy said, "I don't think the snowflakes look like feathers, Mr. Kilpatrick. Each one has a beautiful little design. Look!" Betsy held out her arm, and Mr. Kilpatrick and Billy examined the snowflakes on the sleeve of her red jacket.

"They're pretty, aren't they!" Mr. Kilpatrick said.

"They look just like those glass snowflakes on that Christmas tree we saw this morning," said Billy. "But nobody ever could make them out of snow."

"Snowflakes make themselves," said Betsy, "while they come through the air."

"You don't say!" said Mr. Kilpatrick. "And here I've been thinkin', all these years since I was just a bit of a lad, that they were goose feathers."

Betsy and Billy laughed and looked up into Mr. Kilpatrick's twinkling eyes. "I guess you never made a snowball, Mr. Kilpatrick," said Billy. "You can't make a snowball out of feathers."

"You can't build a snowman out of feathers either," said Betsy.

"Sure! You have no idea what they can do where I come from," said Mr. Kilpatrick. Then he blew his whistle for the traffic to change.

Betsy and Billy went on, but they turned around to look back at Mr. Kilpatrick. They saw him laughing.

As the children walked on, Betsy said, "Oh, Billy! Maybe the snow will last for Christmas!"

"That would be great!" said Billy. "We could go sledding every day all through the holidays."

"Christmas is soon," said Betsy.

"Yepper!" said Billy. "Next week."

When they reached the corner, the children saw something that was a sure sign of Christmas. A big truck was parked beside the curb, and two men were unloading Christmas trees from it. A heavy rope was stretched along the curb between two telephone poles.

Betsy sniffed the odor of the evergreen trees. "Smells like Christmas!" she said.

The children stopped beside the truck to look at the Christmas trees. They were tied together in bundles. One of the men lifted a bundle and cut the strings that bound the trees together. As the trees separated, the man stood them along the sidewalk, resting them against the thick rope.

Billy went to the back of the truck and looked up at the load of Christmas trees. "There are some bigger ones in this truck!" he shouted to Betsy, who was standing on the sidewalk.

"Out of the way, Sonny!" the man on the

truck called to Billy. Billy moved aside as the man threw a bundle of trees down to his helper. "Wonder where Bob is?" he said, as he tossed them down. "He promised to come over and help us."

"I don't know," said the other man. "Sure wish he'd come. I want a cup of coffee."

"Me too," said the man on the truck. "I'm nearly frozen stiff."

"The diner is right across the street," said the other man, as he cut the string on a bundle of trees. "We could keep an eye on the truck."

"I'll watch it for you while you get a cup of coffee," said Billy.

"You will?" said the man, looking at Billy.

"Sure!" replied Billy.

"Hey, Harry!" the man called up to the man in the truck. "This little fellow says he'll watch the truck while we get a cup of coffee."

"And I'll watch the trees for you," said Betsy.

"Okay!" said Harry. "We won't be more than a minute." He scrambled down out of the truck. "Come on, Ray," he said to the other man. "Let's get the coffee."

"This snow sure is coming down," said Ray. "If it keeps up all night, there's going to be a lot of snow on these trees in the morning."

"Never mind the weather, Ray," said Harry. "Let's get the coffee while we have helpers."

The two men crossed the street and went into the diner. Betsy and Billy were alone with the Christmas trees. "I'll stay here behind the truck," said Billy. "You stay there on the sidewalk with the trees."

"What shall I do if someone comes along and wants to buy one?" Betsy called back.

"Sell it to him," said Billy.

"But I don't know how much they are," said Betsy, sticking her head between two trees that were leaning against the rope.

At that very moment the rope that was holding up the trees came untied from one of the poles, and all the Christmas trees fell with a swish into the street. The avalanche knocked Billy over and buried him.

Billy called out, "Hey, help!" Betsy ran to help him.

Christmas trees seemed to be everywhere. They looked much bigger lying in the street than they had standing along the sidewalk. Betsy thought she should run over to the diner and call Harry and Ray.

While she was waiting for the traffic to go by, she saw Mr. Kilpatrick's red car coming down the street. Betsy jumped up and down and waved for Mr. Kilpatrick to stop. The red car slowed down and came to a halt beside Betsy.

"What's the matter?" Mr. Kilpatrick called out.

"Billy's under the Christmas tree!" Betsy called back.

"Under the Christmas tree!" exclaimed Mr. Kilpatrick. "It's pretty early to be finding things under the Christmas tree," he remarked, as he stepped out of his car.

Betsy led Mr. Kilpatrick to where Billy was thrashing around under the branches of a big spruce tree. "Well, I never!" said Mr. Kilpatrick, lifting some of the branches. When he saw Billy's frightened face, he said, "Look what's under the Christmas tree!"

Billy crawled out. He knew that he had not been hurt, but still he was a little scared. "Thanks, Mr. Kilpatrick," said Billy, dusting spruce needles off himself.

"Are you all right?" asked the policeman.

"I'm all right," replied Billy. "I just didn't know what hit me."

At that moment Harry and Ray came running across the street from the diner. When they saw all the Christmas trees lying in the street, they said, "What happened?"

"The rope gave way," said Betsy. "The Christmas trees fell over on Billy."

"That's right!" said Mr. Kilpatrick. "Billy was under the Christmas tree, and Santa Claus didn't put him there."

"Oh, that's too bad!" said Harry. "Are you okay?"

"Oh, sure!" Billy replied.

"Look," said Harry, "here are a couple of little trees. One for each of you. You can have them for taking care of the place for us." Harry picked up two little trees. "Can you carry these?"

"Oh, yes!" said Betsy. "Thank you!"

"You bet!" said Billy. "Thanks a lot."

"Here," said Mr. Kilpatrick, "I'll run you both home. Throw those trees into my car. I'm through for the day." Harry threw the trees into the back of Mr. Kilpatrick's car, and the two children climbed into the front seat.

As they drove away, Betsy and Billy called out to Harry and Ray, "Have a merry Christmas! Thanks for the Christmas trees!"

When they reached Billy's house, Mr. Kilpatrick lifted Billy's Christmas tree out of the car. "Thanks, Mr. Kilpatrick," said Billy. "And thanks for bringing me home."

As Billy dragged the tree up to his front door, Betsy called out, "Good night, Billy! You said this morning you might get your Christmas tree today!"

Billy looked back and laughed. "That's right," he said, "but I didn't expect it to knock me down."

Betsy and Mr. Kilpatrick laughed together as they drove away.

Chapter 9

SOMETHING FOR THE BIRDS

O<small>NE YEAR</small> there was a great blizzard during the week before Christmas. Susan and Neddie Byrd, who were friends of Betsy, had come to spend the weekend. The snow began to fall Saturday night. By morning the wind had blown the snow into drifts. The three children stood at the windows watching the snow fall like white curtains.

By Sunday night the city was almost silent. Deep snow blocked the trains and the buses. Cars were stuck in the streets and on the turnpikes, so Susan and Neddie had to stay on at Betsy's house. The children didn't mind the storm outside, for they played happily indoors.

On Monday morning Betsy woke up early. She saw at once that the blizzard was over. The sun was shining, and it seemed to be brighter than ever before. Betsy got up and looked out the window. The snow was so white it made her squint her eyes. The ice-covered trees and bushes sparkled with tiny rainbows whose colors were fire bright. A cardinal lighted upon a branch of a bush. The bird was the brightest red she ever had seen. On the icy branch, he was as bright as the red-glass birds that hung on the Christmas tree every year. Now a pheasant appeared. A beautiful cock stepped from between two bushes.

Betsy called to Susan, who was still asleep. "Susan, come quick!"

Susan woke up and rubbed her eyes. "What's the matter?" she asked.

"Come see the pheasant!" said Betsy. "He's beautiful!" Susan jumped out of bed and ran to the window. "See!" said Betsy. "He's pecking at the low branches. I wonder whether he's finding anything to eat!"

"Just ice, I guess," said Susan.

"It's terribly cold to eat ice," said Betsy.

"We should make a birds' Christmas tree," said Susan, "and trim it with lots of food for the birds."

"Like what?" Betsy asked.

"Pieces of suet are good," said Susan.

"I don't think my mother has any suet," said

Betsy. "But we have loads of popcorn. Do you think birds like popcorn?"

"Maybe," said Susan. "I know that pheasants like corn, so maybe they like popcorn, too."

Betsy still was watching the pheasant. "I wish I could walk on top of the snow the way that pheasant does," she said. "But I would sink in above my knees."

Neddie came running into Betsy's room in his pajamas. "What are you doing?" he asked.

"Look at the pheasant, Neddie," said Betsy.

"Oh, isn't it pretty!" said Neddie, gazing out the window.

"We're going to make a Christmas tree for the birds," said Betsy. "We can use that nice little tree that is out beside the back door. The man who sells Christmas trees gave it to me."

"What will we hang on the tree?" Neddie asked. "Balls and candy canes?"

"No, of course not!" said Betsy. "What would

the birds do with balls and candy canes? We have to hang food on the tree."

"Birds are just crazy about peanut butter," said Susan.

"How are we going to hang peanut butter on a tree?" exclaimed Betsy.

"Peanut-butter sandwiches?" cried Neddie. "Whoever heard of a Christmas tree with pea-nut-butter sandwiches hanging from it?" He laughed.

"Not peanut-butter sandwiches, Neddie," said Susan. "Just peanut butter."

"Well, I don't know how you can hang peanut butter on a tree," said Betsy.

"You have to put it in something," said Susan.

"Like what?" Betsy asked.

"Well, I know somebody who put food for the birds in a half of a coconut shell. Then she hung it up," said Susan.

"A coconut shell!" exclaimed Betsy. "I'm sure

my mother doesn't have any coconut shells. She buys coconut in boxes."

Star came into Betsy's room in her nightgown with her clothes in her arms. She heard the word *coconut.* "I want some coconut!" she said.

"Coconut is for the birds," said Neddie.

"No, Neddie!" said Susan. "The coconut isn't for the birds. The coconut shell held the food for the birds."

Just then Betsy's mother called up the stairs. "Come, children! Breakfast will be ready soon."

Neddie scampered back to Star's room. Susan ran into the bathroom and turned on the water. Betsy and Star began to dress. Soon the four children were washed and dressed. They ran down the stairs and into the kitchen. "Good morning!" they shouted.

"Good morning!" replied Betsy's mother, pouring orange juice from the squeezer into a glass. Six full glasses stood on the kitchen table. They were surrounded with orange skins.

Susan picked up one of the orange skins. "Look, Betsy!" she cried. "We could hang these on the tree!"

"Orange skins!" cried Star. "Don't want orange skins on the Christmas tree!"

"For the birds, Star!" said Susan. "We can make little baskets and put peanut butter in them."

"Oh, that's wonderful!" cried Betsy. "It's just the thing!" Then she added, "Mother, we're going to trim a Christmas tree for the birds."

"That is nice for the birds," said her mother, "but we have only one jar of peanut butter. Either there is peanut butter for your sandwiches or peanut butter for the birds. You children will have to decide which it will be."

"I love peanut-butter sandwiches," said Star in a sorry voice.

"So do I," sighed Neddie.

"But the poor little birds are hungry," said Susan.

"I'm hungry," said Star.

"Me, too!" said Neddie. "I would like to have a peanut-butter sandwich for breakfast."

"You are having cereal," said Star's mother. "All of you sit down and eat your breakfast."

"Please don't throw away the orange skins," said Susan.

"They are all here," replied Betsy's mother. "All twenty-four halves."

"That's wonderful!" said Betsy. "But we should have more than that."

"First we have to vote about the peanut butter," said Susan, as she sat down at the table.

"Yes!" said Betsy, pulling up her chair. She looked around the table, and said, "All in favor of giving the peanut butter to the birds, hold up your hand."

Betsy, Susan, and Neddie held up their hands. Star just looked into her bowl of cereal.

"Star," said Betsy, "we'll let you help trim the

tree for the birds." Star kept right on looking into her bowl of cereal.

Betsy's father came into the room. "Good morning!" he said, as he sat down at the head of the table.

"Good morning!" the children replied.

"Now," said Betsy, "I'll ask the question again. All in favor, hold up your hand." This time all the children raised their hands. Betsy's father raised his hand, too. Betsy laughed and said, "Why, Father! You don't know what you're voting for."

"I know I don't," her father replied. "I just like to vote for things. Now tell me, what did I vote for?"

"To give up peanut butter for the birds," said Betsy.

"Good!" said her father. "I don't like the stuff anyway. It sticks to the roof of my mouth. Are you sure birds like peanut butter?"

"They love it!" said Susan.

"I'm glad I voted in favor of it," said Father.

"We just have to get more orange skins!" said Susan. "Twenty-four won't be enough to trim the tree."

Betsy's eyes brightened with an idea. "I guess," she said, "if we went over to the Jacksons' right after breakfast, we could get their orange skins. They always have orange juice for breakfast. There is Mr. Jackson and Mrs. Jackson and Clementine and Lillybell. Lillybell," Betsy explained to Susan and Neddie, "is Clementine's little girl."

"Lillybell is my best friend," said Star.

"They have two oranges apiece every morning," said Betsy, "so that's eight oranges, and each one cut in half makes sixteen skins."

"Oh, that's wonderful!" said Susan.

"Then there are Mr. and Mrs. Robinson, across the street from the Jacksons. We can get eight more orange skins there," said Betsy. "We still need more, but they will help."

"Isn't there somebody with five or six children?" Susan asked.

Betsy thought a moment. "Not right around here."

"The snow is so deep," said Susan. "Can we walk to the Jacksons' in it?"

"No," said Betsy. "I guess Father will have to pull us on our sled."

"What's that?" said Father.

"Will you pull us on our sled, Father?" asked Betsy. "So that we can get the orange skins?"

"Orange skins!" exclaimed her father. "Do you mean that you are asking me to pull you around on a sled, while you collect the neighbors' garbage?"

"But Father, it's for the birds," said Betsy. "You voted in favor."

"I voted in favor of giving them the peanut

butter," replied her father. "I did not vote for orange skins."

"But you see, Father," said Betsy, "we can't give the peanut butter to the birds unless we have orange skins."

"Why not?" asked Father.

"Because we have to serve the peanut butter to the birds in the orange skins," Betsy explained.

"Served in orange skins!" exclaimed her father. "And I suppose you are planning to give them napkins and finger bowls?"

All the children laughed merrily. Then Betsy said, "You can't put peanut butter on trees without putting it in something, Father."

"I know that," her father replied, "but I am not going out to collect garbage for the birds!"

"I wish you wouldn't call it *garbage,* Father," said Betsy. "It's just orange skins."

"An orange skin without the orange inside is

garbage," said her father. "If you want to hang *our* garbage on a Christmas tree, very well. But I will not have the neighborhood garbage hanging on the Christmas tree."

"All right," sighed Betsy. "We'll have to use just our orange skins, but they will trim only one side of the tree."

"Well, in this kind of weather," said her father, "half a Christmas tree is better than none."

After breakfast Susan and Betsy scraped the inside of the skins until they were clean. Then they put some peanut butter into each one. They spent the rest of the morning making little cradles of string to hold the orange cups. The girls set Neddie to work stringing popcorn on a heavy thread. Star sat eating popcorn out of the big can. "We'll put some of the popcorn garlands on the birds' tree, and the rest we can save for our own Christmas tree," said Betsy.

While Betsy and Susan were busy making the tasty ornaments for the birds' tree, Betsy's mother was paring apples for applesauce. She pared the skins around and around without breaking them. When she finished, the entire red apple skin lay curled up on the table. When Betsy saw the apple parings, she said, "Oh, we can hang those apple skins on the birds' Christmas tree."

"Oh, yes!" said Susan. "They will hang like icicles."

"Whoever heard of red icicles!" said Neddie, threading his needle through a piece of popcorn.

Not until after lunch was everything ready to be hung on the tree. The children put on their snowsuits, their caps, and their galoshes. Susan carried the basket with the trimmings for the tree in it to the side porch, and Betsy brought the little Christmas tree from beside the back door. The snow was very deep, and the children

sank so far into it that they hardly could walk. Star fell over every time she tried to take a step. They had to choose a spot for the tree near the house, because they couldn't walk very far in the deep snow. They finally stuck it into the snow close to the dining-room window. The snow held the little tree upright.

"This is a good place for it," said Susan, "because we'll be able to see it from the window."

"Yes," said Betsy. "We'll be able to see the birds eating the peanut butter."

"Lucky birds!" said Neddie. "They get all the peanut butter."

"I love peanut butter," said Star, longingly.

Susan and Betsy hung the orange cups on the branches of the tree. Neddie helped to hang the apple parings. Finally Betsy and Susan draped several garlands of popcorn from branch to branch, all the way from the top to the bottom of the tree. When they were finished, the children were very pleased with the birds' Christmas tree. They stood and admired it. The bright orange cups against the dark green branches made the tree very gay.

"It looks like a real Christmas tree," said Susan.

"I'll bet the birds will be very pleased," said Betsy.

"I hope they appreciate our peanut butter," said Neddie.

Betsy's father came out and looked at the tree. "Isn't it a beautiful Christmas tree, Father?" said Betsy.

"Well," said Father, "it certainly is different! It's the only Garbage tree I ever have seen."

Chapter 10

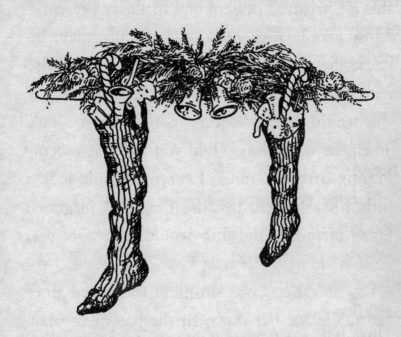

CHRISTMAS CAROLS AND
THE BIRTHDAY TREE

ONCE AGAIN Star had two things to think about—Christmas and her birthday. Because her presents were put under the Christmas tree with her Christmas presents, she always got them mixed up and kept asking all day long, "Is this a Christmas present or a birthday present?" Most people forgot about Star's birthday, because they were so busy thinking about Christmas. When they said, "Merry Christmas, Star," she would reply, "Merry Christmas to you." Then she would say, "Did you know it was my Happy Birthday, too?" Everyone would look a little bit ashamed, because they had forgotten Star's birthday, and they would say, "Oh, yes! So it is! Happy Birthday!"

One day Betsy was sitting at the desk Father had made for her down in the basement playroom. Star came and stood beside her. "What are you doing?" she asked her sister.

"I'm getting my Christmas cards ready to mail," replied Betsy. Betsy handed one of her cards to Star, so she could look at it.

"They're pretty," said Star.

"Yes," replied Betsy. "I always like Christ-

mas cards that show people singing Christmas carols."

"Do they sing 'Happy Birthday'?" Star wanted to know.

"Oh, no!" replied Betsy. "That isn't a Christmas carol."

"I don't see why they don't sing 'Happy Birthday,'" said Star. "It's the little Lord Jesus's birthday, and it's my birthday."

"Well, they don't sing it," said Betsy. "I know, because we're learning Christmas carols at school."

"I know some, too," said Star.

"I'd like to go out on Christmas eve and sing Christmas carols," said Betsy. "It would be fun to go over to Billy's house and stand outside and sing carols. He would be surprised."

"Can I go too?" asked Star.

"Oh, you're too little to go," replied Betsy.

"You couldn't go by yourself," said Star.

"You couldn't sing loud enough all by yourself."

Betsy put her Christmas cards away in a box and said, "Father likes to sing, and he makes a great big noise when he sings. Let's go talk to Mother."

Betsy and Star went upstairs. They found Mother sitting beside the fire in the living room. She was letting down the hem of one of Betsy's dresses. "Mother," said Betsy, "can you and Father go with Star and me to sing Christmas carols on Christmas eve?"

"Where do you want to go?" asked Mother.

"Just over to Billy Porter's house," replied Betsy. "We could stand outside and sing. It would be fun."

"What would be fun?" asked Father, coming into the room.

"We're all going caroling on Christmas eve," said Mother.

"Caroling!" exclaimed Father. "I can't go caroling on Christmas eve. I have to trim the tree."

"Oh, I forgot about the Christmas tree," said Mother.

"How about going out before breakfast, early in the morning?" asked Father.

"Fine!" replied Mother.

"That's a good idea," said Betsy. "I read a story once about some people who went carol singing, and after they sang the people invited them inside, and they had refreshments. So maybe Billy Porter's mother will invite us to breakfast."

"Why, Betsy! Aren't you ashamed of yourself, trying to get a free breakfast," said her mother. "We always have good Christmas breakfasts here."

"Oh, but we don't have those big ginger cookies that Billy's grandmother bakes for them.

Billy says they always have them on Christmas morning for breakfast."

Father interrupted. "Take your mind off cookies," he said. "Tell me where you want to have the Christmas tree this year. Do you want it here in the living room or downstairs?"

"Oh, both!" cried Betsy.

"Can't have both," said Father. "One Christmas tree is enough."

"Oh, we must have it here!" said Mother. "It won't seem like Christmas if we can't open the front door and see the Christmas tree."

Suddenly Star spoke up. "Why aren't there birthday trees?" she asked.

"Birthday trees!" exclaimed Betsy. "Whoever heard of a birthday tree!"

"I think there should be birthday trees," said Star.

Star and Betsy went to bed early on Christmas eve, and Father and Mother set to work trimming the tree. When they had finished they sat down to admire it. The tree stood on the floor, and its top touched the ceiling. Only the lights on the tree were lit. The fireplace glowed with bright red embers. Father and Mother sat beside the fire, feeling its warmth.

In a few minutes, Mother said, "It's the prettiest tree we ever have had."

"You say that every year," said Father.

"It's true," said Mother. "Every year you are a better tree trimmer."

Father laughed. "What about the other tree?" he asked.

"Oh, yes!" replied Mother. "Let's get on with it."

Father put out the lights on the Christmas tree and went outside. In a few minutes he brought a small tree through the back door. "Come along," he said. "It won't take long to trim this one."

Father took the tree downstairs and into the

children's playroom. Mother followed him. Soon
the tree was standing straight and firm in a corner of the room. They set to work again, and the
tree grew more and more beautiful as they
trimmed it. Finally Mother draped a string of
letters across the tree. She had made them herself and had painted them with gold paint. The
letters said, "Happy Birthday to Star."

"We'll put all of her birthday presents under
this tree," said Mother. "This year Star won't
get her Christmas presents mixed up with her
birthday presents." When the tree was finished,
Mother placed seven packages under it. Then
she and Father went to bed.

Very early in the morning, before daybreak,
Betsy woke up. At first she did not know why
she felt excited. Then, suddenly, she remembered. It was Christmas morning! She jumped
out of bed and pulled on her bathrobe. She ran
into Star's room. Star was sound asleep, so Betsy

shook her shoulder. "Star!" she whispered. "Star! It's Christmas, Star!"

Star opened her eyes, and said, "What?"

"It's Christmas!" said Betsy. "Get up! We're going out caroling. Don't you remember?"

Star rubbed her eyes and crawled out of bed, while Betsy went across the hall to Father and Mother's room. "Mother!" she called out. "Isn't it time to go caroling?"

Mother woke up and looked at the clock on the table beside her bed. It was five thirty. "Yes, I guess so," she said.

Father just grunted and rolled over. Betsy shook him. "Father," she said. "Merry Christmas! It's time to go caroling."

Father grunted again. Then he said, "I can't sing this early in the morning." But he put his feet on the floor and sat on the edge of the bed. Then he yawned. "Whose idea was it to go caroling at this hour in the morning?"

"Yours," said Mother. Everyone laughed except Father. He just yawned again.

Before long Betsy and Star and their father and mother were in the car and on their way to Billy's house. It had begun to snow, and their car made the first tracks in the smooth white street.

"Billy is going to be surprised, isn't he?" said Star.

"Yes," said Betsy. "I hope they have those ginger cookies for breakfast."

When they reached Billy's house, it was still dark. As they drove into the driveway, however, Father could see that the garage door was up and the car was gone. "They've gone out," he said. "The car is gone."

"Oh, no!" exclaimed Betsy. "Maybe they're home anyway. Maybe somebody borrowed their car."

Betsy and Star and Father and Mother got out

of the car. They tiptoed up the path to the front door. There was a beautiful wreath tied to the door knocker. Hanging from the wreath was a piece of white paper. Father struck a match and held it so he could read what was written on the paper. He read it aloud. "Have gone caroling," it said.

"Oh, maybe they went to our house," said Betsy. "Let's hurry home."

"Listen," said Father, "you got me out of bed to sing Christmas carols, and now I'm going to sing. If I can't sing to the Porters, I'll sing to their neighbors." Father opened his mouth and began to sing, "Hark the herald angels sing." Betsy and Star and Mother joined in and sang along with him.

When they had finished, windows were opened and voices called out, "Merry Christmas! Merry Christmas!"

"Merry Christmas!" the carolers called back.

"Oh, I hope we haven't missed the Porters," said Betsy. "You think they'll come and sing for us, don't you, Mother?"

"I think they will," she replied.

"Do we have to go back to bed to listen?" asked Star.

"Oh, no!" said Mother. "Now that we're up, we'll stay up. I'll start breakfast, so that we can invite them in."

"It's too bad about the ginger cookies," said Betsy.

When they reached home, the dawn was just breaking. A pinkish glow spread over the eastern sky. "Do you think they've been here already?" asked Betsy anxiously.

"There's no mark of tires in the snow, except ours," said Father.

"That's good," said Betsy.

"Now we'll see our presents, won't we?" said Star.

"Yes," said Mother, as Father opened the front door.

The children ran into the living room without stopping to take off their coats and hats. As Father lit the tree, they both cried out, "Oh! Oh!"

"Oh, it's beautiful!" said Betsy.

Star was already on the floor looking over the packages under the tree.

"Your packages have a big *S* on them, Star," said her mother.

"And mine have a *B*," said Betsy.

"Which are my birthday presents?" said Star. "How do I know which are my birthday presents?"

"Your birthday presents are not there," said Mother.

"Didn't I get any birthday presents?" Star cried.

"Of course, you did," replied Mother.

"They're down in the playroom. It's Christmas up here and birthday down there."

"Oh, let's go see," said Betsy.

The children hurried downstairs. Father already had snapped on the lights. There stood the little tree, hung with nothing but stars and the gold letters.

"Why, it's Star's birthday tree!" cried Betsy.

"Oh!" cried Star. "I've got a birthday tree." She jumped up and down and shouted. "A birthday tree! A birthday tree!"

Just then Father put up his hand, and said, "Listen!"

The children stood beside each other, listening. Voices came from outside. They were singing, "Silent Night." Betsy turned to run upstairs. Father put his arm around her and held her back. "Wait until they've finished," he said.

The two little girls stood clinging to Father as they listened to the familiar Christmas carol. Finally they heard something that surprised everyone except Star. The carolers were singing:

> "Happy birthday to you,
> Happy birthday to you,
> Happy birthday, dear Star,
> Happy birthday to you."

Then they called out, "Merry Christmas!"

Betsy, Star, and Father rushed upstairs. Mother was already at the front door. "Merry Christmas!" she called out. "Come in. Come in."

Mr. and Mrs. Porter and Billy, with Ellen and Linda and their big brother, came into the house. They all were covered with snowflakes. Everyone called out, "Merry Christmas!"

"Star, did you hear us singing 'Happy Birthday'?" said Linda.

"Yes," said Star, her face shining.

"We each brought you a birthday present," said Ellen.

Star was delighted when she saw the packages.

"Oh, thank you!" she cried. Then she said, "I have a birthday tree. It has me all over it."

"What do you mean, it has you all over it?" asked Billy.

"It has stars all over it," said Star. Everyone laughed.

"Here, Betsy," said Billy. "We brought you some ginger cookies."

"Oh, thank you!" said Betsy. "That's wonderful!"

Soon everyone was seated around the breakfast table. "Star," said Mother, "will you say grace?"

"Couldn't I sing a Christmas carol instead?" asked Star.

"Very well," said Mother. "Sing a Christmas carol."

Star looked around the table, and everyone looked at Star. Then she bowed her head and sang:

"Happy birthday to you,
Happy birthday to you,
Happy birthday, Lord Jesus,
Happy birthday to you."

CAROLYN HAYWOOD is distinguished both as author and illustrator of children's books. Her first story *"B" Is for Betsy* was published in 1939. Since then she has had thirty others published and has become one of the most widely read American writers for younger children.

Miss Haywood was born in Philadelphia and still lives in that city. She is a graduate of the Philadelphia Normal School and studied at the Pennsylvania Academy of Fine Arts, where she was awarded a Cresson European Scholarship for distinguished work. In 1969, she was made a Distinguished Daughter of Pennsylvania.

The models for the illustrations in Miss Haywood's books are the neighborhood children who come to her studio and pose for the drawings. She is also a familiar figure in some of the local schools, where she sketches the children during their recess and lunch periods. A portrait painter, Miss Haywood has specialized in portraits of children. Her experience in this field has given her a sympathetic understanding of children and their interests, which has made her peculiarly well fitted to write and illustrate for them.